BRAINWASHED!

R. McGeddon

Illustrated by Jamie Littler

LITTLE, BROWN BOOKS FOR YOUNG READERS
www.lbkids.co.uk

With special thanks to Barry Hutchison

LITTLE, BROWN BOOKS FOR YOUNG READERS

First published in Great Britain in 2014 by Little, Brown Books for Young Readers
This paperback edition published in 2015 by Hodder & Stoughton

3 5 7 9 10 8 6 4

A CIP catalogue record for this book
is available from the British Library.

ISBN 978-0-349-00177-7

Typeset in Minion by M Rules
Printed and bound in Great Britain by
Clays Ltd, St Ives plc

The paper and board used in this book are
made from wood from responsible sources.

MIX
Paper from
responsible sources
FSC® C104740

Little, Brown Books for Young Readers
An imprint of
Hachette Children's Group
Part of Hodder & Stoughton
338 Euston Road, London NW1 3BH

An Hachette UK Company
www.hachette.co.uk

www.lbkids.co.uk

For that creepy guy
standing behind you.
NO, DON'T LOOK!

CHAPTER ONE

KABOOM!

No, that wasn't an explosion. Sorry to get your hopes up. An explosion would have been a smashing way to open the book, but that's not what's happening. It was the sound of a thought arriving in the brain of Sam Saunders with such force it was almost loud enough for the people around him to hear it too.

The thought that *KABOOMED* into his head as he darted across the school playing field was this:

Exercise is excellent.

Now don't get me wrong – Sam isn't one of those weirdoes who loves going to the gym and running on treadmills until they throw up all down themselves. The sort of exercise Sam loves is the running-about-with-yer-mates sort. The wind-in-your-face, isn't-it-great-to-be-alive type of activity.

And it's not like he's forcing exercise down anyone's throat. He isn't wearing a T-shirt that says how excellent exercise is or anything, he's just thinking it inside his own head, and there's nothing wrong with that, even if he is thinking it really quite loudly indeed.

Behind him, one of his best friends, Emmie, hurried to keep up. She also enjoyed running about, but not enough to make a *KABOOM!* noise inside her mind.

Much further behind Emmie was Sam's

other best friend, Arty. From the way he was sweating and panting and dragging his clumping great feet across the grass it was plain for all to see that physical effort was not really Arty's cup of tea. He did not think exercise was excellent. He thought it was a right old load of rubbish and no mistake.

"I'm . . . going . . . to die," Arty wheezed.

Emmie glanced over her shoulder. Arty's face was red and puffed up, like the wrong end of a baboon, so Emmie offered him some words of encouragement.

"Oh shut up, you're not going to die."

"Almost there, Arty," called Sam. "You can do it!"

Up ahead, across the playing field, he could see a group of kids gathering beside . . . someone else. The sun in his eyes made it impossible to figure out who it was.

Sam and Emmie slowed to a jog so as not to leave Arty trailing too far behind. They're nice like that. And people say youngsters have no consideration these days. *Tch*. I dunno.

"It's not fair," Arty gasped. "It's bad enough we have to do PE in school, now I'm d-doing sports club in the holidays."

Sports club was Arty's idea of a living

4

nightmare. It was supposedly started to give the young people of Sitting Duck a fun place to go during the holidays, but Arty reckoned the real reason it was started was to keep them out of trouble. Either that, or the whole thing had been devised as a very elaborate form of torture just for him.

"You'll have a great time!" said Sam.

"I'll have a heart attack," Arty grumbled.

Emmie squinted into the sun as she ran. "Is that Coach Mackenzie?"

"Oh no," Arty groaned. "He made me run until I was sick!"

"How long did that take?" Emmie asked.

"About a minute and a half," Arty wheezed.

Sam shrugged. "He was OK. All those laps he made us do came in handy when we had to run away from the undead. If it wasn't for him we might have been zombie chow."

"I'd rather be zombie chow than be running laps," Arty said. "Please don't let it be him."

"I don't think it is," said Sam. They were getting closer now and the sun was dipping behind a cloud. "Not unless he's got a lot thinner."

"And become a woman," added Emmie.

"I wouldn't put anything past that guy," Arty muttered.

He stopped running. His body gave him no choice. He hobbled onwards, Sam and Emmie slowing down to walk beside him.

"We still going to the town hall after this?" Arty asked.

"The town hall was blown to smithereens by an alien death ray," Emmie pointed out. "Or did you forget?"

Arty sighed. It was tremendously painful and he made a mental note not to do it again.

6

"They're rebuilding," he said. "And they're announcing the candidates standing to become mayor today."

"Why would anyone want to be mayor after what happened to the last one?" Emmie wondered. "Mayor Sozzle was zapped into millions of atoms."

Arty cleared his throat and nodded in Sam's direction. Emmie quickly realised what he was getting at.

"But I . . . erm . . . I'm sure if your dad wins then *he* won't be zapped to atoms," she said to Sam. "I meant the other candidates."

Sam shrugged. "I wouldn't worry about it. The aliens aren't coming back here in a hurry."

"Exactly! Anyway, it's going to be sooooo boring," Emmie complained. "A load of people just standing around talking rubbish about how much better they'll be for Sitting Duck than the rest. How dull can you get?"

"You don't have to come," Sam told her.

"Are you kidding?" cried Emmie. "It's that or I have to go back home and watch Great Aunt Doris chew off her toenails. I wouldn't miss this town hall thing for the world."

"Ooh, hello! New people!" beamed the definitely-not-Coach-Mackenzie person. She was a young woman with short blonde hair and a smile that could crack walnuts across a crowded room.

Actually, I've got no idea what I mean by that. I was trying to say her smile was very nice. I've got no clue how walnuts got involved.

Her eyes sparkled like lemonade, only blue and round and less runny. She wore grey shorts that showed off her legs, like shorts

8

tend to do, and a white T-shirt with the word "COACH" written across the front.

"You're the most beautiful creature I've ever seen," blurted Arty. Around him, the dozen or so other kids sniggered behind their hands. Arty felt his face turn a worrying shade of red. "Er . . . by which I mean 'hello'," he said.

He held out a shaking hand. The coach flashed him a walnut-cracker and shook it. "Pleased to meet you," she said, and Arty knew in that moment he'd never wash that hand again.

Emmie sneered and turned to Sam. "Can you believe the way he's drooling over her?" she asked, but Sam was staring past her, his head cocked to one side, a smile tugging at the corners of his mouth.

Were he a cartoon, Sam's eyes would have been the shape of love-hearts, and he'd almost certainly have been floating several centimetres above the ground. Not being a cartoon, though, he merely stood there with a soppy expression on his face and dribbled very slightly down his chin.

Emmie cast her gaze across the rest of the group. Most of them were boys, and most of them were staring at the coach. Even Brendan Jenkins was staring, and he was blind!

OK, he wasn't strictly speaking blind, but he did have a dog (who will not be appearing in this book. Sorry, pet fans!).

"Welcome to sports club at Hetchley's Park, everyone," the coach beamed. "My name is Coach Priscilla, but you can call me Priscilla. Or Coach. Or Coach Priscilla. It's entirely up to you, really. Whatever you feel comfortable with."

Priscilla gazed round at the faces of the children watching her. "I mean, obviously 'Coach' isn't my actual name, that would be mad . . ." She laughed sharply, making everyone jump. "Just my little joke," she said, cranking up her magical smile so far that somewhere in the world a unicorn spontaneously popped into existence. "Who'd like to have some fun?"

The hands of every boy in the immediate vicinity shot up.

"Great! Then let's start with jumping jacks!"

A chorus of disappointed groans went around the group. Because no one likes jumping jacks, do they? Not even Sam, who thinks that exercise is excellent, remember?

"I love jumping jacks!" cried Jesse, one of the bigger boys gathered near the back of the group. "I love them with all my heart!"

Arty stared at his older brother in horror as he launched into a frenzied fit of arm-flapping. Arty suspected his newfound enthusiasm for jumping jacks had more than a little to do with the coach. Of the two siblings, Arty was definitely the brainy one. Mind you, that's not saying much. Brendan Jenkins' dog (who, I remind you, will not be appearing in this story at any point) was more intelligent than Jesse.

In fact, on a good day there were probably certain types of grass with more smarts than Arty's big brother, but what Jesse lacked in intellect he made up for in his ability to punch people hard in the face.

"That's the spirit," Priscilla cheered.

Priscilla Character Profile

Name: Priscilla

Job: Coach

Appearance:
Aw, just lovely.

Likes: People
shouting
about how
good Sitting
Duck is;
jumping jacks;
freeze tag;
kindness.

Dislikes: People not listening to a word
she says; laziness; nasty people.

Emmie nudged Sam, snapping him out of his trance. "She's nothing like Coach Mackenzie, is she? Jesse would never do those lame exercises for him."

Around them everyone started flapping their arms as they launched into half-hearted jumping jacks. Sam and Emmie sprang into action, immediately competing with one another to see who could do the most. Arty let out a groan and then he did his best to join in, and that's what counts.

"Excellent! All in unison – your town would be proud," the coach gushed. "Now let's do some motivational chanting! Repeat after me, 'Sitting Duck is good'."

The kids looked around at one another. A few of them murmured the words, but then tailed off into embarrassed silence.

"You can do better than that," Priscilla

said. "Come on, Sitting Duck is good. Sitting Duck is good!"

There was something about the panicky desperation in Priscilla's voice that made Sam want to help her. Even though it was really weird, he drew in a deep breath, opened his mouth, and then chanted at the top of his voice.

"Sitting Duck is good. Sitting Duck is good!"

Emmie rolled her eyes, but joined in anyway, because it's important to support your friends, even when they're humiliating themselves. Arty would have liked to join in, but he was too focused on trying not to be sick over his own shoes.

In no time, the whole group had begun to chant along. "Sitting Duck is good. Sitting Duck is good."

Priscilla clapped her hands in excitement.

"Yes! Brilliant! You're doing so well," she cried. "This will be terrific practice."

"For what?" asked Emmie.

Priscilla's smile froze on her face. "Just . . . in general," she said. She quickly brightened again. "Now, let's play freeze tag!"

"What's that?" Jesse asked.

"It's really easy," Priscilla said. "One person is 'it'. When they tag someone, that person then has to stay perfectly still for the rest of the game."

Arty waved his hands. "Ooh! Ooh! Tag me! Tag me first!"

Across the field, somewhere in the distance, the tinkling of an ice cream van's jingle came floating in on the breeze. Suddenly, Priscilla's smile was nudged out of Sam's thoughts by the image of a massive ninety-nine with strawberry sauce.

17

As the coach tried explaining the rules of freeze tag to Jesse for a second and then third and fourth time, Sam gestured to Emmie and Arty to follow him. Side by side they sneaked off across the field in search of ice cream.

"Well she seemed nice," said Arty when they were safely out of earshot.

"Bit weird," said Emmie. "I mean, what was all that 'Sitting Duck is good' stuff about?"

Sam shrugged. "Just building town pride, I suppose."

"Hmm, maybe," said Emmie, rubbing her chin like someone just realising they'd lost their beard. "But, then again, maybe not."

Fun Holiday Games

Bored during the holidays? Why not have a go at one or more of the fun-filled games they play in Sitting Duck? Don't worry if you don't know the rules – make them up and have a try anyway. It might be fun!

Although it probably won't be.

- Touch-face

- King Neptune's Bees

- Who's Stick is This?

- Duck, Duck, Moose!

- Tag

CHAPTER TWO

The town hall – as you might expect of something that had been blown to bits during an alien invasion – was in a right old state.

It was no longer a big crater in the ground, so things had definitely improved, but it still looked rubbish.

At least, all the residents of Sitting Duck who had gathered around it assumed it looked rubbish. What was left of it was hidden beneath a big tarpaulin, a whole lot of scaffolding and a whacking great fence.

A load
of trucks and
vans kept driving in the
gate and through a flap in the
tarpaulin. Look, here comes one now.

HOOOOONK!

Arty jumped out of the path of a
monstrously huge lorry as it swept
along the road and
through the gap
in the

fence. Two towering gates rolled closed behind it.

"Road hog!" Arty shouted, waving a fist at the truck. The high side of the vehicle had been painted with a swirly spiral logo. Arty made a mental note to find out the name of the company later, so he could write a stern letter of complaint.

As he, Emmie and Sam headed in the direction of the gathered crowds, Arty began composing the letter in his head. *Dear Ignorant Buffoons* – that was how it would start. *After that it should pretty much write itself*, he reckoned.

There was a real atmosphere of excitement among the people, who had all gathered to see who would be putting themselves forward to become the new mayor. It was quite impressive that something like that could still get them excited, really, what with all the zombies and the alien invasion they'd all gone through. You'd think everything else would be boring after that sort of thing.

"That's a big tarpaulin," Sam whistled, but no one understood him so he said it using actual words as well.

"I wonder how the rebuild is going," said Arty. "I've heard the designs are really quite breath-taking."

"It's a town hall," Emmie said. "How breath-taking could it be?"

"Why don't we take a peek?" Sam suggested.

Arty's face went pale. "But . . . there's a fence!"

"We could climb over it."

"And . . . and . . . the tarpaulin."

"We could sneak under it."

"And an armed guard!"

"We could . . . Wait," Sam frowned. "Armed guard?"

And there bleedin' well was, too. He approached them slowly, a machine-gun cradled in his arms and a beard nestled on his face.

"Halt," he said, although his heart didn't really seem to be in it. It was like he was looking through them instead of at them. His eyes were slightly glazed, as if he'd recently been hit on the head with a coconut. Or, you know, something else. It didn't specifically have to be a coconut; that was just an example. "Entry is not permitted."

"Why not?" asked Sam.

Arty gasped. "Don't ask him questions, he's got a machine-gun!"

"Why do you have a machine-gun?" Emmie asked.

"And definitely don't ask him that!"

"Entry is not permitted," said the guard again. His voice was dull and robot-like. It went with his eyes. "Disobedience is bad. Obedience is good."

Sam and Emmie exchanged a puzzled glance. "Er . . . whatever you say," said Sam.

"Obedience is good," repeated the guard. "Sitting Duck is good."

A screech of feedback made Sam and the others turn. The deputy mayor was standing on a little wooden box in front of the fence, and smiling nervously down at the gathered crowds.

"Come on, it's starting. Let's go," Arty urged.

With a quick, uneasy glance at the guard, Sam led the rest of them over to join the audience. The deputy mayor patted the pockets of his suit jacket and then pulled out a small notepad. After noisily clearing his throat, he slowly and awkwardly began to read.

"Good morrow, fine people of Sitting Duck," he read. "It's a relief to see you weren't all horribly killed by zombies or aliens before you got here."

Pausing for laughter he looked up

hopefully from his notepad. A sea of stony faces stared back at him.

"No?" he squeaked, then he flipped the page and continued. "Then allow me to start by saying . . . Milk. Eggs. Washing powder. Jam . . ."

The deputy mayor frowned and squinted at the page. "Hang on, no, that's my shopping list."

He flipped another page. "Right. Here we go. As you all know, our much missed and dearly loved former Mayor Sozzle was recently disintegrated by alien dwarves. The time has come to elect a successor, and today we have four fine candidates putting themselves forward."

There was a smattering of applause as the candidates stepped out from the audience. They all tried to huddle together on the deputy mayor's box, which immediately collapsed under their combined weight.

"First up is a man who needs no introduction, but I'm required to give him one by law, so I suppose I'd better," announced the deputy mayor (or the DM as I'm going to call him from now on, because I'm dead lazy like that). "He's old, he used to be in the army, and he's largely responsible for killing half the town when they turned into zombies that one time. Ladies and gentlemen . . . Major Muldoon!"

A grey-haired man with a toilet brush 'tache took a sharp pace forward and fired off a crisp salute.

"Indeed! Tally-ho, what?" barked Major Muldoon. "Blast those zombies, I did, by jove! Took their heads clean off. BANG! BANG! Brains everywhere. You see, you'll always be safe if you vote for me. Make me Mayor Major Muldoon and you can all sleep more soundly in your beds, what?"

"They found a cure, though," called a voice from the crowd. "They'd have been fine if you hadn't blown their heads off."

"You shot my gran," grumbled someone else. "And I'm not even sure she was a zombie."

An unhappy murmuring began to spread through the crowd. The DM stepped up and nudged the major aside. "Next, let's hear from someone with a strong view on education. It's Tribbler the Dribbler!"

Sam, Emmie and Arty snorted out a laugh as their teacher's face contorted in anger.

"No!" yelped the DM. "I mean, *Miss Tribbler*. Not . . . I didn't . . . The dribbling's none of my business!"

"Oh, shut up," snapped Miss Tribbler,

elbowing the DM out of the way. "Greetings friends," she said, and a fine rain of saliva showered the first three rows of the audience. "A vote for Tribbler is a vote for the future. I believe education is key, which is why I'll be introducing compulsory adult education for everyone in town, with double homework at weekends. It'll be utterly fabulous!"

An enterprising member of the crowd began selling overpriced waterproof ponchos to the people around him.

"We don't want to do homework!" protested a voice from the crowd.

"Me am clever enough!" agreed another.

The DM took that as his cue to bring on the next candidate. Before he could introduce her, she snatched the microphone from his hands and flashed a force ten smile at the audience.

"Like, having me as mayor would be *so* awesome," trilled a blonde-haired girl in an expensive designer dress.

Emmie groaned. "Phoebe."

"What's she doing here?" said Sam.

"Vote for me and I totally swear there'll be free spa treatments for everyone," Phoebe shrieked. "Unless, you know, you're way ugly, in which case what's the point? Anyway, if you are ugly – and I can see a few of you in the audience today – I'm afraid you will be asked to leave town."

"Oh, sit down, Phoebe," snarled Emmie. "You're twelve. You're not even old enough to vote, never mind stand for election."

"She, for example, will be the first to go," sneered Phoebe, but then she dropped the microphone when Emmie made a lunge for her, and hid behind Major Muldoon.

The crowd was growing uneasy. The last mayor was bad, but this lot were even worse. Any one of them would be a disaster for Sitting Duck.

"Which brings me to our final candidate here with us today," announced the DM.

"Here goes," said Sam, and he realised he was suddenly feeling nervous as his dad smiled warmly and gave the crowd a wave.

"Samuel Saunders Senior," began the DM. He looked at his notepad and frowned. "Who I don't have any information on whatsoever."

"No, I expect you don't, Mr Deputy Mayor," said Mr Saunders. "You see, I'm no one special. I'm just a husband and a father who loves his town."

The crowd fell silent and listened. Sam felt embarrassed and proud at the same time as

he watched his dad addressing the gathered
townsfolk.

"I believe in Sitting Duck," Sam Snr
continued. "I believe we have something
special here." He pointed to a woman in the
crowd. "Like your electric wig business, Mrs
Winkins. What other town in the country can
boast one of those?"

Mrs Winkins smiled shyly as the people around her clapped her on the back and mumbled their appreciation.

"Or our giant bee statue, made entirely out of smaller bees all glued together," said Mr Saunders. "Or the custard pond. Or trees. Where else can you find those things? Nowhere. Nowhere but Sitting Duck."

"Except the trees," said the DM. "They're quite common."

"But our trees aren't just trees, they're *Sitting Duck trees*," said Mr Saunders, and the crowd cheered at that. "And that makes them the best darned trees in the world!"

The audience was completely on his side now. They hugged one another and exchanged high-fives. Some of them even cried, the soppy fools.

"We live in an amazing place, which is

why the producers of that alien invasion film choose to shoot it here," said Sam Snr.

Emmie leaned closer to Sam and whispered. "Wait, he still doesn't know that was real?"

"Not a clue," said Sam.

"Sitting Duck is amazing," Mr Saunders cried, and the first few rows rushed forward to hoist him up on to their shoulders. "And with your vote I'll do everything in my power to keep it that way!"

Sam watched in amazement as his dad was carried off along the street on a sea of supporters.

"You know," said Arty, "I think your old man might just be in with a chance."

Sam and Arty's Election Pledges

You've heard from the four candidates in the Sitting Duck mayoral election . . . but what if Sam and Arty were running for office? Here are just a few of the promises they'd make to win your votes:

- No homework. Ever.

- No school either for that matter.

- Free games consoles for everyone under 14.

- Adult-free areas of town where grown-ups are not allowed.

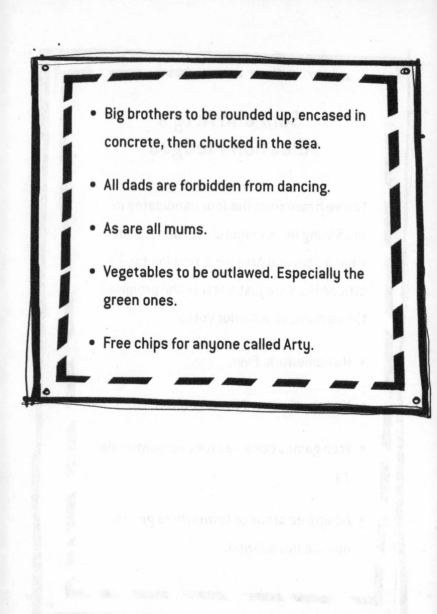

- Big brothers to be rounded up, encased in concrete, then chucked in the sea.

- All dads are forbidden from dancing.

- As are all mums.

- Vegetables to be outlawed. Especially the green ones.

- Free chips for anyone called Arty.

CHAPTER THREE

The next day, Arty ran for his life.

His legs pumped, his chest heaved, colourful spots of light danced before his eyes, but still he ran. Behind him, sharp yellow teeth snapped hungrily at him, closing in with each passing second.

"Dog!" he yelped, hurling himself over a garden gate and landing in a clumsy heap on the pavement.

A bundle of flyers encouraging people to vote for Sam's dad slipped from his bag and began to blow all over the road. Arty hurriedly grabbed for them as, on the other side of the gate, an angry chihuahua yelped and snarled like a wrong 'un.

A car pulled up beside him and Sam hopped out of the back. Sam was wearing a brightly coloured rosette with his dad's face on it. He helped Arty gather up the flyers, then they both hopped back inside the car.

"That was close," Arty panted. Sam's dad turned around in the front seat.

"Wow, sorry about that, Arty," he said. "I really appreciate you helping like this. It wasn't my intention to put you in danger."

Arty nodded. "It's OK, Mr Saunders. I handled it. I eat danger for breakfast."

"And cake," Sam reminded him.

"Oh yeah. I eat danger and cake for breakfast."

BREAKFAST
MENU
FULL ENGLISH
POACHED EGG
DANGER
CAKE
CEREAL

Sam reached over on to the front passenger seat and came back with two megaphones. He held one out to Arty and grinned. "Shall we?"

"Seat belts, boys," said Mr Saunders as he slowly began to drive towards home.

With a *clunk* and a *click* Sam and Arty strapped themselves in, then they wound down their windows, poked their megaphones out, and began to drum up support.

"Vote Saunders," urged Arty. "He's never shot your zombified loved ones in the face."

"Or spat on your children," added Sam.

"And he isn't a twelve-year-old girl," Arty continued.

"Not since the operation, anyway," announced Sam.

"Samuel!" said his dad, but he smiled because he's got a pretty good sense of humour for an adult, which is reason enough to vote for him if you ask me.

"A vote for Mr Saunders is a vote for . . ." Arty began, then he drew a blank. "Er . . . Mr Saunders," he concluded. "Sorry," he whispered. "I probably should have thought that one through."

"Don't worry, Arty, you're doing great," said Sam's dad. "Now let's get back home. The television coverage is about to start!"

Election Tips

Looking to get yourself elected as mayor/
Prime Minister/King of the World? Here are
some tips which may come in handy during
your campaign.

DO smile warmly and naturally.

DON'T grimace like a serial killer and visibly
twitch.

DO kiss voters' babies and throw sticks for
their dogs.

DON'T get these two things mixed up.

DO address voters as 'sir' or 'madam'.

DON'T get these two things mixed up, either.

DO listen to voters' concerns.

DON'T offer them money to shut up.

It was strange for Sam to see his dad on local TV. He was so used to seeing him sitting at the breakfast table in his pyjamas or gardening in his scruffy overalls, that he barely recognised his old man there on screen, all spick and span and looking like a proper grown-up.

Sam and Arty were sitting on the couch, Sam's parents wedging them in at either side. A small group of supporters knelt around the coffee table, drawing posters, designing flyers and making more rosettes. They all gave a little cheer whenever Mr Saunders' name was mentioned on the telly.

Some Sitting Duck residents were being interviewed to get their thoughts on yesterday's campaign speeches.

"So, who will you be voting for?" asked the presenter, thrusting a microphone into the face of a surprised looking man.

"Yes," he said.

"That doesn't answer the question."

The man frowned. "Sorry, can you ask me again?"

"Who will you be voting for?"

The man nodded. "Yes."

The presenter tutted, then turned to someone else.

"Hey, that's that security guard," Sam said, recognising the glazed-over eyes. And the machine-gun.

"Who will you be voting for?" the presenter asked.

"Sitting Duck is good."

"Right. Yes. But who will you be voting for?" asked the presenter, who sounded like she was rapidly approaching the end of her tether. "I mean, it's not that difficult a question."

"Questions are bad," droned the guard. "Obedience is good."

The presenter threw down her microphone. "Oh forget it," she snapped, then she stormed off in a right old huff.

The screen changed to show the bronzed face of local news anchor, Jock McGarry. He raised an eyebrow, waggled his impressive moustache and smiled, showing off teeth so white they actually went *ting* like they do in cartoons. It was amazing, you should have seen it.

Jock McGarry
Character Profile

Name: Jock McGarry

Age: He says twenty-seven. I'd say closer to forty-seven, frankly.

Job: Best Darned News Anchor in the World!

Marital status: Divorced. Eight times.

Likes: Golf, shiny teeth, nodding at important things, Stephanie who does the weather, talking, sitting behind desks and shuffling papers.

Dislikes: Gavin from the sports desk, bad hair days, the price of sunbeds these days.

Ambition: To discover a new type of news. Or to own a puppet. Either one.

"Some interesting insights there, thank you," said Jock, in a voice like warm chocolate. "And now I bring you some exciting election news. It seems a fifth candidate has decided to enter the race to become mayor."

Everyone in Sam's house leaned forward and listened intently.

"Ladies and gentlemen – but especially the ladies," said Jock with a wink. "We now bring you live to the home of renowned scientist, Dr Noah Goode."

A brief burst of static filled the screen, and then an altogether much less attractive man replaced Jock. Whereas Jock was tanned, broad-shouldered and chiselled-looking, this man was pale and skinny (although he did look as if someone had taken a chisel to his face at some point).

One eye seemed to be set a few centimetres

higher than the other. It couldn't seem to agree with the other one on which direction to look either. They both pointed opposite ways as if they'd had a nasty argument.

The man's back was hunched and bent. It bulged up at the shoulders beneath his white lab coat, making him look as if his head was emerging from somewhere in his chest.

It was fair to say he was not a good-looking man, and had Phoebe been there she would almost certainly have been sick out of her nose and fainted, and not necessarily in that order.

"People of Sitting Duck, I am Dr Goode," he began. "For weeks now my teams have been working to rebuild the town hall, utilising state-of-the-art equipment of my own design."

"Hey, I've heard about this guy," said Sam's mum. "Doesn't he live in that old dormant volcano outside of town?"

"What?" spluttered Sam. "There's a volcano in Sitting Duck?"

"Yes, Mount Crumble," said his mum. "I thought everyone knew."

"I did," Arty confirmed.

Sam tutted. "Nobody tells me anything."

On screen, Dr Goode continued his speech. "With my help, though, we can do more than rebuild. We can expand. We can be better than we are. Vote for me in tomorrow's election and I shall not merely give you 'my best', I shall give you the world!"

Sam's dad chuckled. "Typical election posturing, that," he said. "Big talk now, then it all gets forgotten."

"He doesn't have a chance," said Mrs Saunders. "I mean who's going to vote for a creepy old scientist living in a volcano?"

Arty slowly raised a hand.

"Well, fortunately you're not old enough to vote," said Mrs Saunders, ruffling his hair. "Oh no, this isn't a problem. Perhaps if we were electing a new Bond villain he'd be in with a chance, but mayor? I don't think so."

"Yeah, he's just weird," agreed Sam. He got up to turn off the TV, and that's when he noticed that Dr Goode had pulled on a pair of thick-rimmed glasses. They were not a good look for him. If those glasses were a fashion statement, that statement would simply be "No".

Sam reached for the power switch. But, just before he pressed it, on-screen a little antenna popped up from one side of Dr Goode's glasses. The lenses darkened, then began to swirl with a strange spiral pattern. Sam recognised it as the pattern from the truck that had almost flattened Arty.

The mad scientist was still talking –

something about votes and being good – but Sam could now barely hear him. Instead, all his attention was focused on that swirly pattern in the glasses. It seemed to pull him in, drawing him closer and closer to the television. He couldn't take his eyes away; he couldn't hear himself think.

The floor beneath Sam's feet seemed to spin. He felt the ceiling slide away. And then there was the sensation of falling. And then there was a *thud* as he hit the carpet.

And then . . . there was nothing at all.

CHAPTER FOUR

The next day was Election Day! There was bunting! And flags! And a rigidly controlled voting process overseen by a hard-working team of independently appointed officials! It was a fun day out for all the family, if they a) liked that sort of thing and b) were all over eighteen years of age, because a mayoral election is no place for children, thank you very much.

Sam, Arty and Emmie were on their way for another day of sports club. This time

Emmie took the lead, but every time she marched ahead she was forced to wait for Sam and Arty to catch up.

"You see the election coverage yesterday?" Emmie asked. Sam and Arty both grunted in reply. "I only saw the first few seconds before Great Aunt Doris told me that TV was bad for me and sent me to bed. The mad bat said it would rot my teeth."

Emmie looked at the boys, hoping for some sort of reaction. They shuffled on, barely half awake.

"Did you two stay up late watching it or something?" she asked. "You look knackered."

Sam and Arty gave themselves a shake and seemed to come round.

"What?" said Sam. "Sorry, yeah, just feeling a bit out of it today. We did watch the election stuff . . ."

He turned to Arty. "Didn't we?"

"Yes," said Arty. "I mean . . . probably. I'm pretty sure we did. It's all just a bit of a haze."

"That exciting, was it?" said Emmie, smirking. "Glad I missed it."

A car drew up beside them and Sam's dad leaned out. "Morning all," he said. "Have fun at the sports club. That's me off to the polling booth. Fingers crossed!"

"You'll do great," Sam told him.

"Yeah, we have total faith," agreed Arty.

Emmie smiled encouragingly. "Good luck, Mr Saunders."

At that, a glazed expression fell over Sam's dad's face. "Goode is good," he said, his voice little more than a low drone.

"Goode is good," chimed Arty and Sam together. Their faces wore the same glazed expression as Mr Saunders and their bodies

snapped to attention. Emmie felt a shiver run the length of her spine.

"Um . . . you guys OK?"

"Never better," said Mr Saunders, snapping out of it. "See you all later!"

"Bye!" said Arty.

"See ya," said Sam.

Emmie peered at them as Mr Saunders drove off, unsure of what had just happened.

"Er . . . why are you staring at me?" asked Arty.

"What was that about?" Emmie demanded.

"What was what about?" said Sam.

"You went all weird when I said 'good luck'."

Arty and Sam's eyes glazed over once again. "Goode is good," they said. "Goode is good."

"OK, now you're weirding me out," Emmie said.

"Why, what's up?" asked Sam, suddenly back to normal.

"It's like you guys have been brainwashed," Emmie told them. "It sounds hard to believe but then, hey, compared to zombies and aliens it's actually quite normal."

"Brainwashed?" laughed Arty. "Don't be ridiculous. By who?"

"By Dr . . ." Emmie began, but she caught herself in time. "By the fifth candidate in the election."

"You mean—?" began Sam, but Emmie clamped her hand over his mouth before he could get any further. "Don't say it! I think that's some kind of trigger word."

"Dr, um, G. would never try to brainwash us," Sam said, when Emmie had taken her hand back.

"Dr G. loves us," said Arty. "And we love him."

"Now let's get to sports club," urged Sam. "Exercise is excellent."

"No, Sam," corrected Arty. "Exercise is *good*."

"Goode is good."

Emmie stared at Arty in disbelief, as he and Sam headed for the sports field. "OK, Arty looking forward to exercise?" she said, hurrying to keep up, "Now I *know* you've been brainwashed."

Things continued to go downhill for Emmie after that. Not only had her two best friends been hypno-zapped, but Coach Priscilla was up to something too.

Last time Emmie and the others had been there, the boys had all stared at Priscilla with their tongues hanging out, while the girls had crossed their arms, rolled their eyes and generally looked a bit cross.

Today, though, was different. Boys and girls alike lined up before her. They stared not *at* her, but *through* her, just like the guard at the town hall had done.

What's more, last time the group was bored stiff. Now they hung on her every word like a load of really swotty dogs at obedience school.

"Today we shall all be *Goode* citizens," she said.

Everyone responded in unison. "Goode is good."

"Oh yes he is," Priscilla grinned. "Now, drills. One lap around the field, fifty jumping jacks then pull-ups on the climbing frame until I say stop. Go!"

As everyone set off, Emmie pretended to tie up her shoelace. Coach Priscilla was definitely in on whatever was going on, and Emmie was determined to get to the bottom of it.

Before she could question the coach, though, Jesse came darting across the field. He frantically adjusted his hair and did the breathing-on-the-hand test to make sure his breath didn't smell, then he jogged to a stop beside the coach.

"Sorry I'm late," he said. "I got held up. There's some sort of voting thing on or something."

"The election," nodded Priscilla. "The election is good."

"Is it?" Jesse said. He shrugged. "Well, whatever. I'm here now."

"Yes you are," said Priscilla. "And that is *good*."

Jesse's face brightened. "Is it? You think me being here is good?"

The coach smiled. Jesse may not have seen the broadcast, but she still had him completely under her power. "I do. Now run along with the rest of them, there's a good lad."

"Watch me go!" cried Jesse, his muscular legs powering him across the grass. He began to close the gap on the others in a matter of seconds, all the while looking back at Priscilla and grinning like a lovesick schoolboy, which, as it happens, was precisely what he was.

It was then that the coach noticed Emmie kneeling on the ground tying her shoes. Emmie had hoped to get to Priscilla  before the others made it around the field, but Sam and the others were almost back already. Her interrogation would have to wait.

"Why aren't you running?" asked the coach, eyeing Emmie with suspicion. "Running is good."

Emmie hesitated, then she stood up and tried to copy the same dead-eyed expression she'd seen on everyone else. "Goode is good," she chimed.

"Well done," said Priscilla, smiling. "Now get going."

Emmie set off just as Sam and the others were arriving. They immediately launched into the jumping jacks, and it was only then that Emmie realised Arty was there, too. He had somehow managed to keep pace with the rest of them, and there he was, jumping along in perfect time.

By the time Emmie finished her lap, the others were on to the pull-ups. She had barely started her jumping jacks when Priscilla's mobile phone gave a sharp *bleep* in her pocket.

The coach took out the phone, read the

message and then broke into a broad grin. "Good news everyone!" she said.

"Goode is good," they all replied.

"The election is over. We have a new mayor. Dr Goode has won by an absolute landslide!"

"Goode is good!" cheered pretty much everyone except Jesse, Emmie and Priscilla herself.

Emmie sidled over to Sam. "What about your dad?" she hissed.

A flicker of concern passed across Sam's face. "Oh yeah. I wanted him to win, didn't I?" he said. He turned to Emmie and for the first time in as far back as Emmie could remember, he looked worried. "So how come I'm so happy that he didn't?"

HELP! My Friend Has Been Brainwashed!

So a friend or family member has been brainwashed and you're not sure what to do. Have no fear! Here are some possible suggestions for ways you might deal with them:

1. Lock them in a cupboard.

2. Lock them in a different cupboard.

3. Tie them to a tree.

4. Stuff their ears with cotton wool so they can't hear any commands.

5. Remove their eyes so they can't see any commands, either.

6. Actually, forget that last one. Get a blindfold. Much less messy.

HELP! I Want to Brainwash My Friend!

Oh, it's like that, is it? You want to try brainwashing your friend or family member to do your bidding? You naughty person, you. Well, some of these might help . . .

1. Wave your hands about in front of their face and say "Do as you are bid!" in a spooky voice.

2. Jab them repeatedly with your finger while going, "Are you brainwashed yet? Are you brainwashed yet? Are you brainwashed yet?" over and over again.

3. Invest billions of pounds in the development of a state-of-the-art brainwashing hypno-ray device. Or, alternatively . . .

4. Buy a pocket watch on a chain and swing it back and forth before their eyes.

5. Record yourself whispering "You shall obey my every command" and play it on loop while they're sleeping.

CHAPTER FIVE

Time passed, in that way that time tends to do. Morning became afternoon, which became early evening, and you can probably figure out most of the rest on your own.

Twenty-four hours (ish) since everything that happened in the last chapter, Sam and Arty were making their way to Emmie's house. This was most unusual.

Emmie's Great Aunt Doris was not the easiest person in the world to get along with. To describe her as a nasty, vindictive old witch would be to do a grave disservice to nasty, vindictive old witches everywhere. She was the most unpleasant person Sam had ever met, and that included the ones who'd been turned into zombies and had tried to eat him.

They stopped at a kerb, letting four trucks with the spiral-pattern design trundle by in the direction of the town hall.

"What do you think she wants to see us for?" Arty wondered as they made their way quickly but carefully across the road. "She never invites us to her house."

"I'm not sure. She didn't say," Sam said. "She just said it was important."

Now safely across the road, they stopped at Emmie's gate. The garden was overgrown and the path was barely visible through the tangle of grass and weeds. At the other end of it, the door stood silent and imposing, as if daring them to knock.

"After y-you," Arty stammered.

Sam opened the gate with a *creak*, which is a sound a rusty hinge makes, as opposed to some sort of special tool he had to open gates with.

They made their way along the path until the door loomed large before them. Taking a deep breath, Sam raised his hand and was about to knock when—

"WHAT DO YOU WANT?" snarled Great Aunt Doris, yanking open the door. She

glared at the boys with her mad old eyes, and rattled her false teeth around in her mouth. "Is Emmie in?" asked Sam.

"Who?"

"Emmie."

"Never heard of her," snapped Doris, and she began to close the door.

Sam put his foot against it. "She's your niece," he reminded her.

"G-great niece," corrected Arty, who had never been so terrified in his life.

"Great? Great?" cried Doris, and she snorted like a racehorse. "There's nothing great about her. She's a waste of space. Great! She's not even *good*."

At once, all three of their faces took on that empty, hollow expression.

"Goode is good," they mumbled. "Goode is good."

They all blinked and then carried on as if nothing had happened.

"Getchoo foot out of my door," Doris growled. "Unless you want to lose it."

"We'd really like to see Emmie," Sam said. He flashed his most winning smile, the one he saved for special occasions. "Please?"

To Arty's amazement, Doris seemed to soften a little. "She's out back in the shed," she grunted. "But you ain't coming traipsing through here leaving muddy footprints on my carpets. Go round the outside."

"Thanks!" Sam said and he pulled his foot out of the way just as Doris hurled her full weight against the door. There was a *thud* and an "Ooyah!" as her face clattered against the other side.

Avoiding Great Aunt Doris

Sometimes you just have to face Doris head
on, but other times it's entirely possible
you'll want to find a way to sneak past
her. Thankfully, getting past the crazy old
bat isn't difficult. Due to a rare medical
condition, Doris is unable to see the colour
orange. Back when she was first figuring
out how to escape her house, Emmie
used that knowledge to create this Doris
Avoidance Suit:

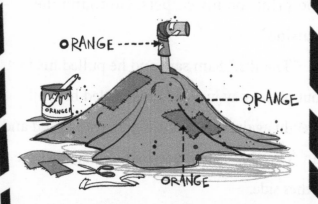

ORANGE

ORANGE

ORANGE

The gap between the side of the house and the fence was narrow, the ground overgrown with prickly bushes and other things no one likes. When Sam and Arty were halfway through the tangle, they spotted Doris's cat, Attila, perched on a fence post like a fat black cat perching on a fence post.

Attila was one of Emmie's greatest enemies, second only to Phoebe. The cat acted like a guard dog, only smaller and more cat-like. He skulked around everywhere, hissing at everyone and attempting to block Emmie's every escape plan.

The cat's eyes narrowed as they drew closer. Attila opened his mouth and let out a hiss.

"Nice kitty," soothed Sam. "Nice little kitty."

But Attila was having none of it. He swiped with his claws right for Sam's face.

Quick as a flash, Sam leaned out of reach, accidentally pulling off a perfect backwards head-butt on Arty.

"Ow!"

"Sorry!"

Attila seemed to smirk for a moment, then he hopped down off the fence and vanished in the undergrowth at their feet. Sam pressed on towards the back garden, with Arty following behind rubbing his aching forehead.

The shed was a ramshackle old thing tucked right away at the bottom of the garden. Sam approached the door and had just raised his hand to knock when—

"What kept you?" demanded Emmie, tearing the door open.

Sam lowered his hand. "Doesn't anyone allow knocking in your family?"

"Come in, quickly," Emmie said. She pulled

them inside, glanced around to make sure they weren't being watched, then closed the door and slid a series of heavy bolts into place.

"What's up?" asked Sam.

"Why are you locking us in a shed?" said Arty.

"For your own goo—" began Emmie, then she stopped herself.

"For our own *goo*?" frowned Arty. "I don't have any goo. At least, I don't think I do have goo."

"For your own *benefit*," Emmie said. She took a heavy hardback book down from a shelf and slammed it on a rusted old workbench.

"Brainwashing for Dunces," Sam read. "Not this again."

"We haven't been brainwashed," protested Arty.

"Goode," said Emmie.

"Goode is good," replied the boys.

"See, why did you say that if you haven't been brainwashed?"

Arty and Sam exchanged a slightly puzzled glance. "I, er, felt like it," said Sam.

"Me too," agreed Arty.

"Yeah, right," snorted Emmie. "Your brains have been well and truly washed by that Dr Goode. Whatever was on that broadcast completely messed up anyone who watched it.

But, don't worry, this book tells me how to fix you. Repeat after me: Goode is bad."

"Goode is good."

Emmie tutted. "*Tch*, so much for that," she said, slamming the book closed. She paced around her friends, looking them up and down.

"I don't get how you two could have been hypno-rayed or whatever so easily," she scowled. "We've fought zombies, defeated alien invaders, and then you just go and let some goggle-eyed old guy make you his puppets. It's disappointing."

"Don't talk about him like that," warned Arty.

"Why not? He *is* a goggle-eyed old guy," Emmie said.

"Well . . . yeah," Arty was forced to agree. "But still."

"And he's controlling everyone like puppets," Emmie continued. "Doesn't sound very good to me."

"Goode is good," droned the boys.

"So you keep saying," Emmie said. "But if that's right, why didn't he help fight the zombies? Or the aliens? He's a scientist, right? He could have given us a hand."

Arty and Sam shifted uncomfortably. "Maybe he was busy," said Sam, all defensive and that.

"Busy designing a hypno-ray or whatever he used to make you his slaves," Emmie said. "I mean think about it," she said. "The guy lives inside a volcano! Name one genuinely good person who lives inside a volcano."

"Goode is . . . good," said the boys, but they sounded much less convinced than they had just a moment ago.

"And what about your dad, Sam?"
Emmie pressed. "You wanted him to win.
Think of all that work you put in trying to
help him."

Sam's eyebrows knotted in the middle, like
two caterpillars having a fight.

"My . . . dad?"

"*And* did you know the lovely Coach
Priscilla is his daughter? Oh yes, I looked it
up. They're in cahoots," said Emmie, then she
said the word "cahoots" again because she
really quite liked it.

"They're up to no good," she concluded.
"And we need to stop them."

"Goode is good," both boys said, but they
sounded *really close* to not actually believing
it.

"He stopped your dad becoming mayor!"

"Goode is . . . good?" said Sam.

"She made you run laps and do jumping jacks!"

"Goode . . . is . . . good," said Arty, grimacing.

"And you enjoyed it, Arty!" Emmie cried. "You enjoyed it!"

Arty's eyes widened. He let out a sharp gasp. "The *monster*!"

Sam blinked. "Hey, wait a minute. Goode is . . ." He gave his head a shake. ". . . Bad. Goode is bad."

"He brainwashed us!" Arty yelped.

"Used us like puppets," said Sam.

"And he'll do the same thing to everyone else in town," Emmie said. "Unless we stop him."

How to Fix a
Brainwashed Best Friend

Oh boy. So a friend or family member has been brainwashed. First of all, you should try not to panic. Actually, forget that. Panic. Panic lots. There's probably no way of getting them back, I'm afraid.

Oh, all right. One of these might snap them out of it.

1. Point out that only really nasty wrong 'uns go about brainwashing people all the time, and that they don't want to be under the command of a wrong 'un.

2. Slap them across the face with a fish.

3. Remind them of how they used to be. Try to do one of their favourite activities with them.

4. Put live spiders down their trousers.

5. Look at photographs of you and your friend together in happier times.

CHAPTER SIX

Sam, Arty and Emmie tiptoed through the
streets of Sitting Duck. Then they realised
they looked daft, and walked properly
instead.

All through the town, speaker systems
had been installed. One had been attached to
the roof of the roof shop. Another had been
fastened to the Zip and Button Emporium,
and the walls of the ice cream cone store were
covered in them.

The speakers were being put up by . . .

well, everyone, really. Dozens of townsfolk clambered up ladders, or shimmied up drainpipes, or formed human pyramids in order to mount the megaphone-like devices nice and high.

None of them said a word as they worked, and Sam and the gang found themselves surrounded by an eerie, unsettling silence.

"What are they up to?" Emmie wondered.

"By the looks of it they're installing a sound system across the whole town," Arty said.

"So either someone's planning a music festival," said Sam. "Or else . . ."

A screech of feedback blasted out from all of the speakers at once, forcing everyone to cover their ears, which did the guy at the top of the human pyramid no favours, let me tell you.

When the din had faded another sound emerged from the speakers – a continuous tone that rose and fell in pitch, and wobbled a bit in the middle. It was an odd sound. A curious sound.

A hypnotic sound.

As one, all of the nearby townsfolk turned and began marching in the direction of the town hall. Emmie moved to follow, but Sam held her back.

"Wait," he hissed. "Listen."

Emmie listened. At first, she heard nothing, but then it came creeping into her ears like some horrible insect: a steady *thud, thud, thud* that quickly grew louder.

All three kids slunk back into the shadows of a doorway as the street was suddenly filled

by an army of Sitting Duckers. They marched
in perfect formation, their eyes glazed, their
faces all slack and droopy.

Signs Someone You Know is in a Hypno-Trance

- Their eyes go all wonky

- They say the same thing over and over again

- They say the same thing over and over again

- They say the same thing over and . . . oh, you get the point

- They walk like their pants are too small

- They talk like a robot

- They do everything a Supervillain says, even if it's really nasty

"We should follow them," said Arty, as if the others couldn't have figured that one out for themselves.

And so they did. It took a while, though, so please enjoy this poem about a cat until they get there.

A cat, a cat,

Is nice an' that,

But sit on it,

And it goes quite flat.

Moving stuff, eh? And the kids have just arrived, so the timing couldn't have been better.

Everyone in Sitting Duck had gathered outside the building formerly known as the town hall. They were jammed together like a forest of trees, as if they weren't quite sure how they'd got there.

A speaker, which had been attached to the

fence by a particularly acrobatic old woman on a trampoline, crackled into life. The same wobbly sound emerged, and the gathered townsfolk snapped to attention.

At the front of the crowd, a very familiar (and quite pretty, if you liked that sort of thing) young woman stepped up on to a box and smiled her winning smile.

"Goode is good," said Coach Priscilla.

"Goode is good," chanted the crowd.

Sam turned to Emmie, keeping his head and his voice low. "You were right. They are in cahoots!"

"Cahoots!" agreed Emmie.

"Cahoots," said Sam again, because it really is quite a fun word when you say it out loud, even dead quietly.

"People of Sitting Duck," Priscilla continued. "Show your love, appreciation and undying loyalty for my father and your new Supreme Overlord, Dr Noah Goode!"

The audience applauded, whistled, made "oooowooo" noises and stamped excitedly on the ground. "Goode is good!" they cheered. "Goode is good!"

Priscilla stepped down from the box, making way for Dr Goode. He waved and nodded at the adoring crowd, then raised both arms for silence. Instantly, a hush descended.

"I think you meant . . . *Mayor* Goode," he said, and the crowd went crazy again.

Goode motioned for silence once again, and once again the audience instantly obeyed. Dr Goode pointed his lumpy big face their way and twisted his mouth into something that was supposed to be a smile, but looked more like a sneeze waiting to happen.

"Now that I have you all under my complete control," began Goode, then he gave a little snigger and slapped himself on the hand. "Naughty. I meant to say, now that you have elected me to represent you all as mayor, I shall deliver on my campaign promises."

Another cheer went up from the crowd. "Goode is good!"

"Although to keep things interesting, I thought we might mix it up a bit. Originally, I promised to give you the world, but now I think I'd like *you* to give it to *me*."

Sam, Emmie and Arty swapped some worried looks.

"Tell me he isn't going to say what I think he is," Arty whispered.

"Look at him," said Sam, gesturing over to the misshapen madman in his lab coat. "Of course that's what he's going to say."

"Wait for it . . ." said Emmie.

Dr Goode drew in a deep breath. "You, my Sitting Duckers, will be my army . . ."

Sam sighed. "Man," he muttered. "I hate it when I'm right."

". . . An army with which I shall conquer the entire world!"

Dr Goode Character Profile

Name: Noah Goode (Dr)

Age: Between 45 and 95, it's hard to tell.

Job: Supervillain, Evil Science Division.

Known Associates: Priscilla Goode (daughter)

Likes: Being mad, making things, plotting, scheming, blowing stuff up, turning things into other things for no real reason, laughing maniacally, brainwashing people for personal gain.

Dislikes: Being foiled, buffoons, shoddy workmanship, things that don't turn into other things no matter how hard you try, wasps.

Ambition: TO RULE THE WORLD! (Did you really have to ask?)

CHAPTER SEVEN

"What do we do? What do we do? What do we do?" fretted Arty. It was the next morning, and he was pacing anxiously around the inside of his tree house, leaving a slug-like trail of terror-sweat behind him.

"Calm down," said Emmie. "Now's not the time to panic."

"Everyone's been brainwashed by a mad scientist with plans for world domination!" Arty reminded her.

"Yeah, fair point," Emmie conceded. "It's probably the ideal time to panic."

After the rally, Mayor Goode had been whisked off somewhere, whilst Priscilla controlled the crowds. Sam, Arty and Emmie had hidden amongst them until they could sneak off back home.

"You know what we need?" asked Sam. He was sitting by the window, gazing through the leaves at the rooftops of Sitting Duck.

"A miracle?" guessed Emmie.

"A false beard and a jetpack?" suggested Arty.

Sam shook his head. "A plan. We need a plan." He turned from the window and looked at his friends. "I mean, obviously it's going to be up to us to stop this. The adults of this town are useless."

"You're right. It's almost like we're the main characters in a series of stories," said Emmie, who could be really quite perceptive sometimes.

"And what excellent stories they'd be," added Arty.

"I agree, they *would* be excellent, and I would highly recommend them to readers of all ages," said Sam, "but now's not the time for that. We've got a town to save! Again."

"So what's the plan?" asked Arty, who was still secretly holding out for the false beard and the jetpack.

Grabbing a rusty nail from the windowsill,

Sam began to scratch a map out on the wooden floor with quite uncanny accuracy. Unfortunately, it was a map of Belgium, and so of no use to them whatsoever.

He dropped the nail, turned to the others and began to reveal his plan.

"Remember my mum saying he had a hideout in Mount Crumble?" he said. "Whatever he's up to, it all started there. If we can get in, we might be able to find a way to stop him."

"I'll go!" said Arty. "I've always wanted to see inside a mad scientist's laboratory."

Emmie crinkled her nose in disgust. "Ew."

"Laboratory," repeated Arty. "Not lavatory."

"Someone should hang about in the town and keep an eye on things. See what Dr Goode and his daughter are up to," Sam said.

"I could do that," Emmie shrugged.

Sam shook his head. "No, too risky. I think Priscilla suspects you weren't affected by the brainwashing. If she sees you she'll get suspicious."

"Well I'm not hiding up here," Emmie said.

"Go with Arty, then. You can protect him."

Arty looked hurt. "I can protect myself!" He considered this for a second. "Actually, no I can't, can I?"

"So it's settled," Sam announced. "You two check out the lab, I'll check out the town. We'll keep in touch by text."

Emmie nodded. "Don't get brainwashed," she told him.

Sam nodded back. "Don't get killed."

"What?" spluttered Arty. "Killed? Why would we get killed?"

"We won't," said Emmie. "Probably."

"Yeah," said Sam. "You're only breaking into the volcano lair of an insane scientific genius. Seriously, what's the worst that could happen?"

*

Sam skulked along the streets, keeping an eye on things and watching out for nonsense. Everyone was going about their business as normal. Shopkeepers kept their shops, innkeepers kept their inns, and beekeepers sold honey that was nice, if a bit on the expensive side.

Up ahead, Sam's dad stepped out of the paper shop, which immediately fell over and blew away. Mr Saunders smiled when he spotted his son, and Sam smiled back because it would have been rude not to.

"Hey, Dad!"

"Hi Sam," said Mr Saunders. "What you up to?"

"This and that," Sam replied. "What about you?"

"Not sure," said Sam Snr. "Just sort of milling about and not really sure why. It's like

I'm waiting for something, but I don't know what." He laughed. "Sounds silly, I know."

"Ha ha, yeah," said Sam, forcing a laugh. "Really silly. Anyway, Dad, I was wondering if . . ."

There was a screech from the nearest speaker, then that weirdly wobbly tone started to drift down the streets of Sitting Duck. Mr Saunders' eyes glazed over in an instant.

"Goode is good," he said, and Sam could hear the same sentence repeated by everyone within earshot. "Goode is good."

"Come to me, people of Sitting Duck," commanded a voice Sam recognised as Priscilla's. "Come and lend your allegiance to Mayor Goode."

"Goode is good," droned the townsfolk. "Goode is good."

Mr Saunders about-turned and joined the

throngs of other Sitting Duckers who were all making their way back to the town hall. Sam had no choice but to follow. The crowd swept him along like a big river of people who have been brainwashed.

"So here we are again," Sam said with a sigh. "If it isn't zombies or aliens it's a power-crazed super villain threatening the safety of everyone in town." He shook his head. "Sometimes I think we should all just stay in bed."

The crowd surged on towards the under-construction town hall. This time, though, they didn't stop by the fence. The gate had been thrown wide and they pushed in, jostling and bumping Sam, and giving it all that, "Goode is good" stuff in his ear.

Beyond the gate they headed towards the big tarpaulin. Sam caught a glimpse of his dad up ahead somewhere, as the tarpaulin was lifted enough for everyone to duck underneath.

When Sam made it through to the other side, he clattered straight into the guard with the machine-gun.

"Oops, sorry," he said, and then from the corner of his eye he saw Coach Priscilla. She turned to look at him suspiciously.

Sam let his eyes glaze over. "Goode is good," he said.

"Goode is good," replied the guard.

Priscilla gave a nod and then turned away. Sam shuffled past the guard and got his first look at the town hall.

ONLY IT WASN'T A TOWN HALL!!!!!

Didn't see that coming, did you?

Where the town hall should have been was a tower of steel girders. It stood a couple of storeys high, wide at the bottom and tapering to a point at the top. Townsfolk clambered over it like insects, screwing in bolts and hammering in studs. The tower looked like the little transmitter that had popped up out of Goode's glasses, only many times bigger and not attached to anyone's face.

Major Muldoon was perched near the top, moustache bristling, eyes glazed, whacking a bolt with a great big spanner.

"Goode is good," he droned.

Arty's brother, Jesse, was up there too. He was attempting to knock in some rivets with a spoon, which was going about as well as can be expected, really. His eyes were also glazed over – but then that was his normal look, so no change there.

"Priscilla is lovely," he muttered. "Priscilla is lovely." Sam began to suspect that Jesse wasn't brainwashed at all, at least not using the same method everyone else had been. He was already brainwashed by Priscilla; maybe you couldn't be brainwashed twice. He worked tirelessly, though, lugging steel and tightening bolts and battering stuff with his spoon.

KA-LANG!

The echo of metal on concrete reverberated around inside the tarpaulin, making Sam's teeth vibrate. All eyes turned to Tribbler the Dribbler, who had accidentally let one of the iron bars topple to the floor.

With a gesture from Priscilla the guard
with the gun stepped forward. He turned the
barrel towards the Dribbler and Sam felt the
world grind into slow motion. He raised his
hand. He opened his mouth. But before any
sound could emerge a crackle of blue energy
spat from the gun.

As the blast struck Miss Tribbler, she
froze. Literally. At first it looked as if she was
sporting some rather dashing glass slippers,
but the ice quickly climbed and spread across
her body until she was encased from head to
toe.

With a satisfied nod, Priscilla gestured
for the guard to get back to work looking
menacing. Sam realised there was another
guard standing beside the coach, ready to do
whatever she bid.

The Sitting Duckers, who had watched

the freezing of the Dribbler, turned back to their work as if nothing had happened. Sam ducked into the shadows and took out his phone.

Freeze guns, he thought. *Hypno-rays.* These were no average villains he was dealing with. Dr Goode was a fully paid up evil genius.

His thumb jabbed at the buttons as he started to write a text but before he could finish, the phone was knocked from his hands. It bounced on the ground with a *crack* and the screen went dark.

Sam looked up. His face fell. His eyes widened.

"You!"

How to Be . . . Brainwashed

You're stuck in the middle of a brainwashed mob, trying to avoid detection while you attempt to bring down their leader. We've all been there. Luckily, blending in isn't difficult with this cut-out-and-keep guide.

DO copy what everyone else is doing.

DON'T do anything different.

And, er, that's about it. It's probably not worth cutting out, really.

What, I never said it was going to be a long guide, did I?

CH★PTER EIGHT

Emmie and Arty pedalled up the steep winding path that led to Mount Crumble. Fortunately for Arty he had built a completely silent electric motor into his bike some weeks previously. As far as everyone else knew the bike was completely normal, but the motor meant that Arty was able to keep up with Emmie without his lungs exploding or his legs falling off.

The trip hadn't started well. Arty had a rough idea of where the lab was supposed to be, because he really embraces all that nerd stuff, and he knows where most of the science-y stuff in town is. The problem was that people kept getting in the road.

Hundreds of them, there were. Thousands. *Hundreds of thousands*, even.

Actually, no, that's too many. Let's stick to hundreds.

They filled the streets with their glassy, doll-like eyes and their lurching, I'm-under-an-evil-scientist's-hypnotic-command-like walks. They shambled in their ranks through the streets, all massing towards the centre of town.

Unfortunately for Arty and Emmie, they were trying to go in the opposite direction with two clunking great bikes, and what should have been a speedy cycle out on to the open road became a long-winded battle through a whole load of brainwashed people.

But all that, like Sitting Duck itself, was now behind them. The path zigzagged up a steep incline, forcing Emmie to pedal harder and Arty to secretly change gear.

"Cor, it's hard work, this," he said, the pedals spinning his legs around without any real involvement from him whatsoever. "Not much further now, though."

He wasn't wrong (but then, he rarely is). As soon as they had crested the hill, Mount Crumble lay directly ahead of them. It rose from the ground like a big mountain with the top cut off. Wisps of grey smoke drifted from the hole in the top, and once or twice a minute the volcano made a noise like an elephant sighing.

"It's not going to blow up on us, is it?" Emmie asked.

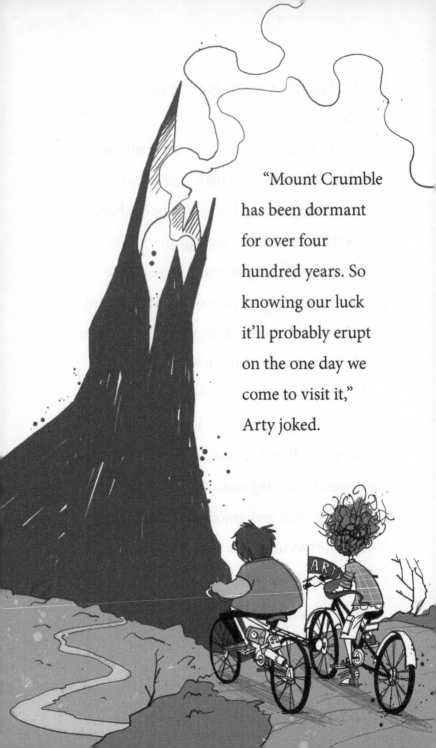

"Mount Crumble has been dormant for over four hundred years. So knowing our luck it'll probably erupt on the one day we come to visit it," Arty joked.

The Greatest Supervillain Lairs . . . Ever!

Over the years, Supervillains have come up with some pretty amazing places from which to carry out their evil deeds. Here are a few of my personal faves.

Villain: The Magpie

Lair: A vast nest situated at the top of a towering Canadian redwood tree, from which the Magpie could swoop down and steal the jewellery of unsuspecting lumberjacks, until one of them chopped it down.

Villain: Baron von Fishy-Wishy

Lair: Von Fishy-Wishy's lair was cunningly hidden inside the belly of a blue whale. This meant the villain could travel throughout the world's oceans, carrying out evil in all its diabolical forms. Unfortunately, he could never find a way to steer, and no one has any idea where he or his lair ended up.

Villain: The Kangaroo

Lair: This pint-sized Australian villain didn't have the wealth or resources to build his own lair, so he took a tip from his animal namesake and set up shop in one of his mum's pockets. Things went pretty well for the Kangaroo for a while after that, until his evil reign was brought to an end when his mum put the coat he was hiding in through the wash.

There was a sudden *BEEP* from Emmie's phone.

"Message from Sam," she said.

"What does it say?"

"*Followed trucks. Snuck under tarpaulin. You won't believe it, but—*"

"But what?" Arty asked.

"Dunno. It ends there."

She fired off a quick reply – "*But what?*" – then slipped the phone back in her pocket.

"What now, then?" she asked. "How do we get inside the base?"

Arty puffed out his cheeks. "Find the entrance?"

"Well *obviously*," Emmie tutted. "But how do we do that?"

Arty thought for a moment. "We could follow the massive truck, I suppose."

Emmie frowned. "What massive truck?"

A massive truck swept past them on its way towards the mountain.

"Oh. *That* massive truck." Emmie noticed

the spiral pattern on the side, the same one they'd been seeing all over town.

They cycled after it, Emmie's legs pumping, Arty's motor whispering along. They rounded a bend and suddenly the massive truck was lost in a crowd of other massive trucks. They thundered in and out through an arched hole with giant metal shutters, built into the mountainside, throwing up clouds of black volcanic dust with their tyres.

A procession of the trucks trundled towards the town. Arty and Emmie bounded down from their bikes and took cover behind a clump of bushes before anyone could ask them who they were, what they were up to, and why they weren't all brainwashed 'n' that.

"I bet the lab is through there," said Arty.

"Oh, *you think*?" snapped Emmie.

Some guards were
standing just outside the entrance,
glassy eyes scanning for trouble. "How do we
get in?" Emmie wondered.

"There's a truck," said
Arty.

"There are loads of trucks," Emmie pointed out.

Arty gestured to one that had stopped just ahead of them. It was a small flatbed, with a bit of tarpaulin covering the back. "I meant that one. We could sneak on the back then hop out when we're inside."

"Good idea," said Emmie.

Arty looked taken aback. "What? Really?"

"Yes. You go first, I'll keep watch."

Arty's face fell. "Me? But I thought I might just wait out here . . ."

Emmie gave him a shove. "Go."

"Right, yes. I suppose," Arty fretted. He glanced around to make sure the coast was clear. "Here goes," he whispered, and then he ran.

And then he got tangled in the bush.

And then Emmie helped untangle him.

And then he ran again.

Heart pounding, blood pumping, bladder quivering nervously, Arty dragged himself up on to the back of the flatbed and covered himself with the tarpaulin. He turned to Emmie and gestured for her to come.

As Emmie took her first step, there was a deafening *roar* and Arty felt the world lurch sharply. His first thought was that the volcano had erupted, and he was about to be smothered by millions of tonnes of molten rock.

His second thought was, "Oh no, the truck's moving." He wasn't entirely sure which thought was worse.

Emmie sprinted flat out, but it was no use. Arty could only watch her fall further and further behind as the truck pulled off and carried him towards the volcano.

Alone.

How to Infiltrate a Secret Base

You've stumbled upon the lair of a Supervillain and you want to peek inside. Before you rush in, brave hero, here are some suggestions that might help.

1. Before attempting anything really clever, check if the door's open. You'd be surprised how often it is.

2. Likewise, check the windows. Supervillain lairs can get quite stuffy, and often the windows will be wide open for most of the day.

3. If the door is locked, check under the mat for a spare key. Keep your eyes peeled for plastic-looking rocks positioned conveniently nearby, too. A key may be lurking inside.

4. Disguise yourself as an evil robot salesman and talk your way inside.

5. Disguise yourself as an evil robot and blast your way inside.

6. Become invisible (trickier than it looks).

7. Pretend to be a photographer from *What Supervillain* magazine, and that you've come to do a two-page spread on the villain's HQ.

8. Um . . . dig a big tunnel or something? I dunno. I'm out of ideas. Write your own below.

9. _____

10. _____

"You!" Sam said again, for the benefit of everyone who forgot he said it at the end of Chapter Seven.

"I think we've established that now," said Priscilla. The coach was no longer smiling a smile that could crack walnuts. She was scowling a scowl that could crack heads. "And as you're clearly not under our control any longer, allow me to say this . . ."

She raised her phone to her mouth and her fine features became twisted with rage. "GET HIM!" she screeched, and her words spat from the speakers positioned around the building site.

All at once, the people of Sitting Duck turned in Sam's direction. They downed their tools and dropped their metal bars.

Then they picked them up again, because they looked much more menacing that way.

CHAPTER NINE

Sam glanced across the crowd. The faces looked familiar but the expressions didn't. Everyone – every single person working on the transmitter – glared at him like he was a bug in need of a-squashin'.

Sam, despite being the bravest person I've ever met, swallowed nervously and flashed a worried smile. "Can we talk about this?" he asked, then he ducked as a claw hammer whistled towards his head. "I'll take that as a *no*," he said, then he shoved Priscilla out of

the way, dodged past an old
lady swinging a brick at him,
and began to run.
Sam twisted,
weaved, rolled,

somersaulted, crawled, cartwheeled,
backflipped, crab-shuffled and wriggled his
way through the throngs of brainwashed

townsfolk. Spanners were swung, hammers were hurled and monkeys were notable by their absence.

Major Muldoon came lunging, swinging with an iron bar. Sam ducked. The bar sliced through the air above Sam's head, then collided with Miss Tribbler – who had recently begun to thaw – knocking her out cold.

With one of those fancy kick-flip things they do in martial arts movies, Sam was back on his feet. With a yank on Major Muldoon's 'tache, Sam sent him spiralling into the path of some more pursuers.

That left the route to the edge of the tarpaulin clear! Sam sped towards it, pulling over a stack of tools behind him.

"STOP HIM!" Priscilla screeched, but Sam was too close to the tarp's edge now. Freedom was just moments away . . .

And that was when things *really* started to go wrong. Dozens of brainwashed Sitting Duckers flooded in below the tarpaulin, weapons raised and faces nasty. Sam jumped sideways just as one man swung with something big and painful-looking.

There was a *crackle* of energy and Sam felt the air beside him burn with cold. The man froze instantly, his weapon still raised to attack. Sam turned in time to see one of Priscilla's guards taking aim with his freeze-ray again.

"This just gets better and better," Sam grimaced. He took cover behind a stack of metal girders just as the guard opened fire. The metal instantly froze, then shattered like glass.

Frantically, Sam looked around. He was blocked in on all sides by people who had been his friends and neighbours. Now they were nothing but drone-faced puppets (which, incidentally, would be an amazing name for a band).

Left, right, forward and back were cut off, so that left Sam with only one route: up. Hurling himself on to the scaffolding he began to climb.

He had almost reached the first platform when Phoebe's face appeared over the edge. "Goode is, like, *totally* good," she chanted, and then she swung an arm down. Sam felt a burst of pain as a mallet thumped against his fingers. His grip slipped and he tumbled backwards on to the concrete floor.

But it would take more than a sore hand and a bruised bottom to stop Sam Saunders! He bounded to his feet! He turned sharply! He stopped immediately as a gun was shoved right up in his face.

On the other end of the weapon stood Priscilla. His eyes met hers, and she flashed him a wicked grin. "How's about a game of freeze tag?"

Slowly, being careful not to be shot in the face by a crazy villain, Sam raised both hands. "OK, you've got me," he said. "But you won't get away with this."

"Oh no! Oh goodness! Oh heavens! We *won't*?" yelped Priscilla, then she let out a snort of laughter. "And who's going to stop us exactly? You? You don't have a hope."

Sam pulled himself up to his full height and squared his shoulders. He looked really quite impressive and grown-up for someone his age, and the circle of brainwashed townsfolk seemed to shrink back a pace.

"I've faced a horde of zombies. I've sent alien invaders packing," Sam said, jabbing a thumb in the direction of the towering metal construction behind him. "You lot can't even build a town hall properly. Of course I can stop you."

"Idiot," Priscilla hissed. "We don't need a town hall any more. Any fool can see that we've been building a transmitter. We just needed an army of volunteers to put the finishing touches on it, and that's where Sitting Duck came in. With that transmitter my father will be able to broadcast his message across the whole world."

A smile crept across Priscilla's face. "Imagine it – his hypnotic signal beamed from country to country, city to city, town to town. Every single person on Earth, all under his command, doing his bidding, bending to his will." She shook her head and sneered. "And you thought we were building a town hall!"

Sam shrugged. "Actually, I didn't," he said. "I knew this was a transmitter, I just didn't know what it was for. Now I do. Thanks for revealing your plan. That'll make it much easier to stop you."

Priscilla's face fell and her cheeks blushed. "No matter," she seethed, raising the gun. "Knowing the plan won't do you any good, because you won't be around to see it put into action!"

And with that, she fired.

The REAL Priscilla Character Profile

Name: Priscilla Goode

Job: Supervillain's daughter

Appearance: Aw, still lovely.

Likes: Evil; shouting; pointing guns; bossing everyone around; villainy; helping take over the world; bubblegum.

Dislikes: Goodness; democracy; children; anything starting with the letter H (don't ask); being nice; singing; joy.

Ambition: TO (help her dad) RULE THE WORLD!

CHAPTER TEN

Arty bounced around on the back of the flatbed as it trundled its way towards the entrance to Dr Goode's volcano lair.

Emmie had left him. He couldn't quite get his head around that. Sam was the bravest person Arty knew, but Emmie . . . Emmie was *fearless*. She never had to be brave because she wasn't really scared of anything, but Arty had just seen her turn and leg it back into the bushes like a smelly coward.

And now he was heading straight into the lion's den, all on his own, with no idea what he was going to be facing. He thought about jumping off, but the truck was moving quite quickly now, and he realised he had two choices: a) Jump off and probably die, or b) Stay on and probably die.

They were not, he realised, great choices.

Suddenly, there was a rustle from the bushes and a shape exploded out through the leaves.

"Emmie!" Arty cheered, then he quickly clamped his hands over his mouth in case anyone heard him.

With a soft, barely audible whine from its electric motor, Arty's bike came speeding up towards the truck, Emmie bent low over the handlebars. She blinked in the cloud of dust and ash being thrown up by the lorry's wheels. Her feet pumped furiously on the pedals, doubling the speed of the motor.

She was gaining! Arty could hardly believe it. Despite the truck's head start, Emmie was closing fast. He held a hand out as she drew up to the back of the vehicle, but Emmie was never very good at accepting help.

With a wobble, she put one foot on the seat, then the other.

The bike slowed so it was no longer gaining, but merely keeping pace with the truck, Emmie now standing upright on the seat.

And then she jumped, like a diver leaping off the board. She sprang through the air and landed expertly on the back of the lorry just as it swept through the arched hole in the rocky mountainside.

She slipped beneath the tarpaulin beside Arty just as two huge metal doors slammed closed with a *clang*.

"Cool electric bike," she whispered.

"What, you mean you knew?"

"Of course I knew. There's no way you could have pedalled up here without help. Besides," she added, "it says 'requires forty-eight AA batteries' on the side."

The truck squeaked to a stop. The engine gave a final shudder as it was shut off. Emmie

and Arty kept quiet as they heard the driver
get out and close his door.

They waited until they could no longer
hear his footsteps before lifting the corner of
the tarpaulin and peeking out.

The inside of the volcano looked pretty
much exactly like you'd expect the inside of a
volcano to look, only with lots of lights, dozens
of people and a fleet of trucks added in.

Arty gazed in wonder at the lights. They
were made up of a network of glass tubes,
stretching all the way from the floor and criss-
crossing across a metal ceiling overhead. Lava
pumped through the tubes, casting a twinkling
orange glow across the cavern-like interior.

"Oh, that's clever," Arty said.

"Yeah, don't you just love what he's done
with the place?" Emmie said, then she slapped
Arty across the back of the head and gestured

to a guard who was marching back and forth in front of a door. "I'm going to go knock him out," she said.

"Why?"

"So I can steal his uniform and disguise myself," she explained. "Then we can find someone else, knock *them* out, too, steal their uniform and—"

"Or we could just wear these," Arty suggested. He held up two overalls that had been bundled up beside him.

"Or we could just do that," conceded Emmie, even though she had been quite looking forward to knocking someone out.

They quickly pulled the overalls on and Arty spent the next minute or so moaning that the material was a bit rough for his delicate skin. Emmie then spent the following minute explaining exactly what she was going to do to him if he didn't stop complaining.

Arty stopped complaining.

They made their way across the cavern towards the door with the guard. It's always a safe bet that the key to defeating the villain will be behind the guarded door rather than, say, on a well-lit plinth with *STEAL ME* printed on it in shiny letters.

All around them, other people in overalls hauled tools and metal into the backs of the waiting trucks. They moved in the now-familiar robotic way, arms jerking, legs shuffling as if they'd wet themselves.

"Act brainwashed," Emmie whispered. She and Arty shuffled their way towards the door. The guard barely even glanced their way as they approached and pushed on through.

Closing the door, they found themselves

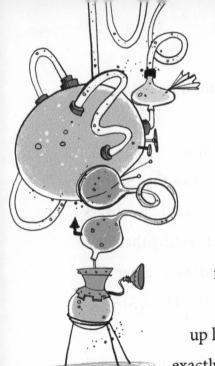

in a long and winding corridor hewn from the rock. Doors and windows lined both walls, and as they crept along they stole fleeting peeks inside.

The first room was set up like a science lab. It was exactly what Arty had always hoped a mad scientist's laboratory would look like. He pressed his face against the glass and gazed longingly inside. Test tubes bubbled with glowing green liquids, pink goo *glooped* along lengths of coiled plastic piping, and one of those electric things that sits in the corner and goes *fzzzzzt* sat in the corner and went *fzzzzzt*.

144

"Cor," said Arty, before Emmie dragged him away.

The other rooms were similarly full of weird and (to Arty, anyway) wonderful stuff. In one room there was a big glass tube containing a chicken with the head of a bear. In another there was a bit of a robot and a diagram showing how to make a kitten massive.

Arty would have loved the chance to explore properly, but they had a job to do, even if they weren't entirely sure what that job was.

"What are we even looking for?" Emmie asked.

"Some way to stop Dr Goode," Arty guessed. "You know – gadgets and stuff."

They stopped at another door. The words *GADGETS AND STUFF* were printed on the nameplate. "They must be in here," said Arty, in what was probably the most obvious statement anyone had ever made in the history of the world ever.

A glance through the window told them there were no baddies lurking in the room, so they hurried inside.

They found all sorts of gizmos scattered across the room's stainless steel worktops. Arty could only guess how they all worked and exactly what they did. He picked up something that looked like a small torch and flicked it on. A blinding light hit him in the face, and he suddenly had an overwhelming desire for a cool, refreshing glass of a famous cola-based drink.

Arty blinked and turned the device over in his hands. A small rectangular label told him it was a *Subliminal Advertising Ray*. He set it down again, and tried to resist the urge to go swimming in a lake of fizzy cola goodness.

"Look at these," said Emmie. She showed Arty a pair of spectacles with swirly lenses, just like the ones Dr Goode had worn on TV. "Think they're important?"

Arty nodded. "I think they might be," he said.

"I'm going to take them," Emmie said, slipping them into her pocket.

"Great plan!" agreed Arty, a little too excitedly. "Then we can go and find a drinks vending machine!"

Emmie frowned. "What?"

Arty gave himself a shake. "Forget it. Doesn't matter."

"We should keep looking," said Emmie. "See if there's anything else."

"Good idea," Arty agreed, but a sudden sound from behind stopped them in their tracks.

The door to the gadget room eased open with a low *creeeeeeak*. Arty and Emmie spun round to find a shadowy figure silhouetted in the doorway.

"Wh-who's there?" Arty gasped.

"I'm every bad dream you've ever had."

The misshapen new mayor of Sitting Duck hobbled from the shadows, glowering at them with his boggly eyes.

His thin lips contorted into a nasty smirk. "Or should that be 'every *Goode* dream'?"

Other Stuff in
Dr Goode's Base

- A big laser

- An even bigger laser

- A rabbit with crab legs

- A crab with no legs

- A detailed plan for creating an
  unstoppable army of ducks

- A *Supervillain of the Year* runner-up
  trophy from 2003

- A lake of acid filled with acid-resistant
  killer penguins

- A *World's Best Dad* mug

CHAPTER ELEVEN

A buffoonish big lump of a shape wrapped around Priscilla just as she opened fire on Sam. The shot went wide, freezing one of her own guards to the spot.

Priscilla growled and wriggled as Jesse hoisted her off the ground. The gun clattered to the floor at Sam's feet. He snatched it up quicker than it took you to read this sentence.

"I love you Priscilla," cried Jesse. "I love you, you big power-crazed maniac, but I can't let you do this!"

"Let me go!"

"Not until you stop being a crazy person," Jesse said. "And when you do, will you marry me?"

"Of course not!" Priscilla growled. Jesse's shoulders sagged.

"Oh right. That's a pity," he said, then he dropped her. She had just enough time to let out a little yelp of panic before her face smacked off the concrete floor. Before she could get back up, Sam had the gun pointed at her face.

"Don't move," he warned.

Priscilla's eyes closed and her shoulders began to shake. At first, Sam thought she was crying, but then he realised she was doing just the opposite.

"Idiot boy," she laughed. "Look around you."

Sam's eyes darted left and right. The townsfolk loomed around him, their weapons raised and at the ready. There was no way he could take them all on, even with the gun.

"You're vastly outnumbered. Even if you do manage to freeze me, you won't accomplish anything. Face it," she sniggered. "You've lost. One push of one little button and the whole world will fall at my father's feet."

"OK. You're right," Sam admitted. "I give up. You win and . . . LOOK AT THAT PUPPY!"

Even through their hypnotic haze, the crowd was powerless to resist the urge to turn and look, because everyone loves a puppy.

Grabbing Jesse, Sam barged his way through a knot of Sitting Duckers, scattering them like skittles. The boys were barely halfway to the tarpaulin when everyone realised there was no puppy, and that it had all been a cruel trick.

"AFTER THEM!" screeched Priscilla.

Mrs Winkins made a desperate lunge for them, twirling one of her electric wigs above her head. Squeezing the trigger of his stolen gun, Sam froze her to the spot.

The deputy mayor came at them next. He grabbed for the gun, but a right hook from Jesse sent him spiralling to the floor.

On they went, zapping and punching their way through the throngs, clearing a path to the exit. "Under, quick," Sam urged, firing randomly back at the closing crowd as Jesse ducked out below the tarp.

Dropping to the floor, Sam rolled out after Jesse, and they both set off at a sprint before the mob could give chase.

"So you weren't brainwashed?" Sam asked, glancing back over his shoulder.

Jesse shook his head. "Only by Priscilla's beauty," he sniffed, wiping a tear from the corner of his eye. "I loved her so, so much."

"*Bleugh*," said Sam, pretending to vomit. "You're gross."

They realised no one was following them and slowed to a stop. Something was happening to the tarpaulin. It seemed to be billowing upwards like one of those Chinese lanterns that keep causing fires everywhere.

"Oh, what now?" muttered Sam, and then

the tarp rose up and was carried off on the wind.

With a series of *clangs* and *boings* the townsfolk toppled the scaffolding, and the transmitter was revealed in its full glory. It towered like a towering thing, all shiny metal and satellite dishes and wires poking out here, there and everywhere.

"Hey, where did that come from?" wondered Jesse.

"Seriously?" sighed Sam. "You were helping to build it five minutes ago."

"Was I?" Jesse frowned. His chest puffed up with pride. "I made a pretty good job of it, too."

A wobbly droning sound began to emanate from somewhere near the base of the transmitter. Circles and spirals of pink light popped and fizzed from the antenna's tip, lighting up the sky and making the clouds glow.

"Oooh," Jesse whispered. "Did I do that, too? Because that's really impressive."

"It's started," gasped Sam. "She's turned on the transmitter. Goode's going to start his broadcast to world. Everyone will be under his control!"

"Goode is good," droned a hundred voices from worryingly close by. Sam and Jesse turned to find a crowd of townspeople had crept around behind them as they watched the light show.

Sam opened fire, freezing half a dozen of them before they could move. Emmie's Great Aunt Doris came shambling out of the ranks. Jesse swung with a powerful uppercut, but Doris moved surprisingly fast for a largely house-bound OAP. She dodged sideways, then *whanged* a frying pan across the side of Jesse's head, knocking him to the ground.

Two figures made a grab for Sam. He turned, finger on the trigger, and came face to face with his mum and dad. He hesitated, just for a moment, but it was a moment too long. The crowd closed in. The gun was torn from Sam's fingers.

And in a frankly terrible turn of events, he was trapped.

World-Conquering Gadgetry

What? You want to take over the world?
Brilliant! We can work together. With our
combined skills no one will be able to stop
us. Those fools won't know what hit them!
Mwahahahahaha!

Oh, wait. You just wanted to find out about
the sort of gadgets someone *might* use to
take over the world? Ahem. Yes. Sorry. Just
my little joke there . . .

1. Hypno-Ray: It's a classic, but it's a classic
   for a reason. All will bend to your will with
   this mesmerising bit of hardware.

2. Freeze-Ray: Again, a well-established
   piece of kit. Freeze your enemies so they
   can't escape! Just try not to drop them
   afterwards or they might smash.

3. Speed-Shoes: Heroic types giving your problems? Take care of them at lightning speed with the help of this super-speed-granting footwear.

4. Hat of Lightning: The enormous metal rod on this cast-iron hat will act as a perfect conduit for bolts of lightning. One blast and you'll gain powers far beyond those of mortal men! Or third degree burns. It's 50/50, really.

5. Solar Drill: Want to carve a hole right through the sun, doom us all to eternal darkness and plunge us into a new ice age? The Solar Drill is what you're after! (Requires solar panels to function.)

CHAPTER TWELVE

Despite being the prisoner of a deranged scientist bent on world domination, Arty was having the time of his life.

After Dr Goode had discovered Emmie and him, he'd pointed a really rather nasty-looking gun their way and marched them towards what would turn out to be his control room. Arty and Emmie stood there now, Emmie glaring at Dr Goode, Arty gazing around in wonder.

Twelve enormous TV screens covered the

walls, each one the height of a double-decker bus. In the centre of the room a hologram of the Earth just floated there, minding its own business, happy as you like. Arty really wanted to ask how it was done, but he thought now probably wasn't the right time.

A small red light *blipped* on and off

roughly above where Sitting Duck would be on the globe, and Dr Goode did an embarrassing little dance of delight when he spotted it. "Yes!" he cried. "Yes! My global hypno-relay is finally complete. Priscilla and the worker-drones of Sitting Duck have done me proud! Now I am free to transmit my message all over the world."

"Let me guess," Emmie seethed. "Would that message be 'Vote Goode'?"

The villain let out a burst of snorting, snuffling laughter, like a badger with a scratch 'n' sniff sticker. "Vote? *Vote?* Why would I bother with a vote?" he giggled. "The election was merely a test to see if my technology worked, and to keep this little town under my control."

Madness blazed behind the doctor's goggly eyes. "And it did! The hypno-relay will beam me into every electronic device in the world. From now on there will be no voting. There will be no rules but mine, no rulers but me. The people of the world shall become my slaves – just like the inhabitants of Sitting Duck – and they will love me for it."

He smiled wistfully and crossed to a leather chair that was positioned in front of a video camera. He rested both hands on the chair's curved back.

"All the world's resources will be mine. Think of the stupidly elaborate gadgets I can build. Think of the needlessly cruel experiments I can conduct. Think of the ridiculously expensive secret lairs I can construct in pointlessly dangerous places!"

"Sounds terrible," Arty lied. He actually thought it sounded quite interesting.

"Once you are under my thrall you will

come round to my way of thinking," Goode said. He patted his coat pockets. "And now, if you'll excuse me, I have a broadcast to make. I just need to . . ."

He patted his trouser pockets.

He felt the top of his head.

A look of panic tried to navigate across his badly arranged face, got lost, and ended up at his elbows instead.

"What's up?" asked Emmie innocently. "Lost something?"

"My . . . my glasses. Where are my glasses?"

"Wait, I know!" said Arty, then he yelped when Emmie kicked him in the shins. "I mean . . . no idea," he grimaced.

Reaching into his lab coat, Dr Goode pulled out what looked like a ray gun. He took aim at Arty's head, which was freakishly large and so not a difficult target. "You know," he barked. "You know where they are."

"He doesn't," said Emmie, as Arty babbled incoherently in complete and utter terror. "But I do."

Dr Goode shot a glance in Emmie's direction and let out a gasp of despair when he saw she was wearing the glasses. "No!"

With a flick of a switch, the little antenna popped out of the frame and the lenses began to swirl. Dr Goode felt a tingly lightness creep

through his retinas and up into his big mad brain. He tried to turn the gun on Emmie, but his arm would no longer obey. His eyes glazed over as he stared into the swirling vortex of the hypno-lenses.

"Put the gun down," Emmie commanded.

Dr Goode put the gun down.

"Slap yourself in the face."

Dr Goode slapped himself in the face.

"Quack like a duck."

"*Quack, quack, quaaaaack!*"

Emmie laughed. "These are brilliant," she said. "I'm so keeping these when we're done."

Arty, who had just about recovered from his fright with the gun, smiled weakly. "Sh-should we save the world first?"

Emmie gave a shrug. "Yeah, might as well," she agreed. She turned to Dr Goode and the swirly pattern of the spectacles' lenses seemed to swirl even faster. "It's time to make your broadcast, Dr Goode."

"It's time to make my broadcast," Dr Goode agreed.

"But I'm going to tell you *exactly* what you're going to say."

"Tell me exactly what I'm going to say," the scientist chimed.

"And make him do something embarrassing," Arty added.

Emmie sucked air in through her teeth. "Arty, that's a terrible thing to suggest," she said. "As if I'd be so cruel . . ."

Two minutes later, Dr Goode sat in front of the video camera, broadcasting his message to the world, and wearing a pair of spotty underpants on his head.

"People of Earth," he droned. "I am now broadcasting on every electronic device across the globe. My name is Dr Noah Goode . . . and I have been a vewy naughty wittle boy."

Behind the camera, Emmie and Arty exchanged a high-five, then went back to watching Goode's brainwashed broadcast.

"I have placed the people of Sitting Duck under hypnotic command in order to make them elect me as their mayor, even though I look funny and smell and am completely evil and everything," Goode continued. "I now relinquish all control and free them from my brainwashing badness."

He stood up, revealing to the world that he was wearing nothing below the waist but a pink tutu and some badly-fitting tights.

"And now," he said, "I shall dance for your amusement."

As the evil scientist began to twirl and spin and pirouette with the grace of a hippo on stilts, Emmie and Arty turned to one another and smiled.

"Well," said Arty, "I'd say that all went really rather well."

"Yeah," agreed Emmie, as they watched Dr Goode skip and dance around the room. "I just hope Sam didn't get himself into too much trouble."

Other Uses for Hypno-Glasses

- Convincing parents to keep you off school.

- Convincing teachers you really did hand in your homework, and it was excellent.

- Convincing school dinner ladies you don't have to eat . . . whatever that stuff is.

- Making everyone think it's your birthday – every day.

- Persuading toy shop owners you won all their stock in a competition.

- Making bullies beat themselves up for a change.

- Keeping the sun out of your eyes.

CHAPTER THIRTEEN

"You killed Sam!" bellowed Jesse, lashing out at three men who were struggling to hold him down. "You monsters, you killed Sam!"

"No they didn't," said Sam, who was at that moment being pinned to the ground by a broad-shouldered woman who worked in the school tuck-shop.

"Oh, right," said Jesse, calming down almost immediately. "Who am I thinking of, then?"

Firm hands hauled at both boys' arms and

legs, holding them in place. A shadow passed above them, and there was Great Aunt Doris glaring down, twirling her frying pan in her hands. From that angle, Sam could see right up her nostrils, where a whacking great clump of hairs sprouted like a rainforest.

"She's going to smash us in the face with that frying pan, isn't she?" sighed Jesse.

"Probably," Sam nodded.

"It's going to hurt, isn't it?"

"Probably," Sam nodded.

Jesse's voice became choked with emotion. "Listen, if you get out of this and I don't, I want you to pass on a message to my little brother for me."

"Of course. What is it?"

With a sharp twist, Jesse wrestled an arm free. He thumped Sam on the upper thigh, giving him a dead leg. "That," Jesse said.

"You're all heart," Sam groaned, and then Doris was bringing the frying pan up, up, up . . .

And then down, down, down . . .

And then Sam's mum was there, her hand grabbing for Doris's arm and spinning the old bat around to face her.

"No one clangs my son in the face with a frying pan!" snapped Mrs Saunders, and Sam saw a flicker of something pass across her face.

In fact, it was passing across all the faces in the crowd. Life was returning to their expressions and the light was returning to their eyes.

The weight on Sam's limbs eased off (although the throbbing in his leg would hang around for days afterwards), as everyone stood up and began muttering in confusion.

"What's going on?"

"What were we doing?"

"Where'd my frying pan come from?"

Sam let out a laugh of relief. "They did it. They actually did it!"

"Who did what?" asked Jesse. He and Sam helped one another to their feet as the crowd drifted away in dribs and drabs.

"Emmie and Arty, they cancelled out the brainwashing," Sam cheered. He pointed up to where the hypno-transmitter was doing absolutely nothing at all. "See?"

"Wait," Jesse frowned. "So Arty saved us from a lifetime of slavery?"

Sam nodded. "Yup!"

Jesse rolled his eyes. "Oh great. I'll never hear the end of that."

Through the thinning crowd they spotted Priscilla making a run for it. Sam began to hobble after her. "Stop! Get back here!"

A blast of cold air gusted past him and Priscilla froze to the spot. Sam turned to see Jesse wielding the freeze-ray. "Not so fast. You're not getting away from me that easily!" Jesse hollered, then he trotted over to Priscilla's side.

Beneath the veneer of ice, her eyes

swivelled until they locked on his big grinning face. "Now you're frozen you'll have to listen to why we should get married. I've written a poem about how I feel."

Jesse reached into his pocket and pulled out a folded up sheet of paper. Priscilla let out a muffled groan of dismay.

"Priscilla, Priscilla, you smell like vanilla," Jesse began, "but you're scary and violent, a bit like Godzilla . . ."

Sam wandered away, nodding and smiling at the people he passed, who were no longer making even half-hearted attempts to kill him. Which was nice.

He passed through the fence, which had been trampled by the angry mob and into the shadows beneath the transmitter. The pink lights still fizzled and flickered across the antenna's tip. Clearly it was still broadcasting *some* sort of message, just not the one the Goodes had been planning, he guessed. He wondered what it was. If he knew Emmie, it would be something pretty spectacular.

Sam kicked around in the dirt until . . . yes, there it was, just where he'd dropped it. He picked up his mobile phone. There were two texts from Emmie. One had come earlier in reply to his half-finished one.

The other text had just come through

a few moments ago, though: "Mission accomplished?"

Sam turned and took a photo of the frozen Priscilla, who was still being subjected to Jesse's poetry. He sent it to Emmie and then slid the phone into his pocket.

"Mission accomplished," he said to nobody in particular, and with a skip in his step Sam Saunders headed for home.

Top 5 Uses for a
Frozen Supervillain

- Door stop

- Garden gnome

- Scarecrow

- Climbing frame

- Sledge

Top 5 Uses for a
Frozen Supervillain

- Door stop

- Garden gnome

- Scarecrow

- Climbing frame

- Sledge

CHAPTER FOURTEEN

Moths passed.

Sorry, *months* passed. My mistake.

The Goodes were thrown in jail, which Priscilla was actually quite happy about, because Jesse wasn't allowed to visit (although he does still send her a new poem every week, bless his heart).

The transmitter was torn down at great expense to the town, which meant there was no money left over to build a new town hall. With Sam's help, though, Mr Saunders was able to convince the townsfolk that they themselves could do the building work. After all, if they could build a state-of-the-art broadcasting antenna (although no one could quite remember why they had) then they could build a town hall!

He was half right. The town hall was . . . unconventional to say the least. No one had really bothered to plan the job out, and everyone had just set about using their own initiative.

As a result, the town hall had one window and nineteen doors. It had three floors, but no stairs or lift, and someone had nailed the roof on upside down.

Yet no one seemed to mind, and everyone was bustling with barely-contained pride when the ribbon was cut and it was declared open for business.

But I'm getting ahead of myself. Let's skip back to just before the opening ceremony, to when an even more important announcement was being made. The deputy mayor of Sitting Duck stepped on to his little wooden box, cleared his throat, and addressed the gathered audience.

"Ladies and gentlemen, the counting has been done and the results are in," he said. "Sitting Duck has a new mayor – who hopefully won't be trying to brainwash us any time soon."

Behind the deputy mayor, the four candidates shuffled nervously from foot to foot.

"In fourth place, with absolutely no votes on account of her not actually being in the election because she's too young, Phoebe Bowles."

"Ha!" shouted Emmie from somewhere in the crowd. Phoebe's face turned an unpleasant shade of purple and she stormed off in a huff.

"Like, who cares about your stupid voting thing?" she scoffed, then she burst into tears and had to be led away gently by a nice woman with a tranquiliser gun.

"In third place, with no votes . . . Tribbler the Dribb—Er, Miss Tribbler!"

"This is a disgrace!" seethed Miss Tribbler, and half of the audience was immediately soaked to the skin.

"In second place," began the DM, then he paused for an agonisingly long time because he'd watched far too many Saturday night TV talent shows and he was dragging it out as much as possible. "With zero votes, so it wasn't actually a close run thing at all really, I just said that for dramatic effect . . ."

In the audience, Sam crossed his fingers. Arty and Emmie put their hands on his shoulders and held their breath.

"Major Muldoon," announced the DM. The crowd went wild, forcing him to shout to make himself heard over the clapping and cheering. "Meaning our new mayor by a unanimous landslide is Sam Saunders Senior!"

"Yes!" yelped Sam Jnr.

"He did it!" whooped Emmie.

"And without a hypno-ray in sight," Arty cried.

The DM stepped aside, allowing Mr – sorry, *Mayor* Saunders to step up on to the box. The cheering rose in volume, and it took several minutes for it to die down enough for Sam's dad to be heard.

"Blimey," he said. "I . . . I don't know what to say."

He reached into his pocket and pulled out a bundle of typed notes. He looked them over, then scrunched them up and tossed them over his shoulder.

"You see, I had a speech prepared just in case I won, but I seem to remember Mayor Goode being a big fan of speeches, and although I'm not entirely sure why, my instincts tell me I don't want to be anything like him."

Another chorus of cheers went up. The memories of those who had been brainwashed were hazy at best, but they all remembered enough to know they weren't fans of Dr Goode either.

"I want us to put the past behind us and move forward together," Mr Saunders continued. "He wanted to be mayor to makes things better for himself. I want to be mayor to make things better for all of us."

The DM handed Mr Saunders a set of comically oversized scissors. Everyone watched in hushed excitement as he approached the ceremonial ribbon that had been strung between the least lopsided of the nineteen door frames.

"We can accomplish incredible things together," Mr Saunders said. "Together we built this place, and together we can build a better Sitting Duck, one that will be disaster free!"

More cheering! More shouting! More other enthusiastic noises I can't think of!

"And so it gives me great pleasure to declare the new Sitting Duck town hall open for business!" Mr Saunders announced. He smiled at the audience as a sea of cameras flash-flash-flashed. He raised the scissors. He snipped the ribbon.

And the entire town hall folded in on itself like a house of cards.

"Disaster free, eh?" whispered Emmie.

"The calamitous town of Sitting Duck?"
Arty laughed.

Sam grinned. "Yeah," he replied.

"Something tells me he may have spoken too
soon on that one . . ."

EXTRACT FROM
SITTING DUCK DISASTER
AVOIDANCE PLAN

In order to increase likelihood of future disasters being averted in the future, it is recommended that in the future we learn from our mistakes and try to avoid the following:

- Reanimating the dead.

- Making our whereabouts known to aliens.

- Accidentally building a massive brainwashing transmitter in the middle of town.

- Likewise, we should – in the future – make every attempt to avoid:

- Summoning a demon.

- Building a robot witch.

- Angering cows.

- Constructing a load of bombs, then later misplacing them.

- Opening a doorway through time.

- Designing a weather machine and programming it to hate us.

- Losing our car keys.

DEFEAT DISASTER WITH YOUR ULTIMATE SURVIVAL HANDBOOKS!

Disaster Diaries: Zombies!

Have you read all of the Disaster Diaries? Read on for a sneak peek at another book in the series . . .

In the sleepy town of Sitting Duck, three fearless friends are about to face a horde of the living dead, who are desperate to munch on braaaaaaaiiiins!

With all the useless adults quickly getting themselves infected, Arty, Sam and Emmie have to take charge.

If they can't find a cure, they'll be zombie breakfast . . .

How to Identify a Zombie!

Think someone you know might secretly be a zombie? Here are some clues to watch out for.

- Their face is hanging off.

- They're trying to eat you.

- They smell like a granny's armpit.

- They walk like someone's stolen their knees.

- They moan a lot (and not about the state of your bedroom – that's probably just your mum).

- Flies follow them everywhere and worms have parties in their hair.

- Their eyes are really creepy (Emmie made me add this one).

Hiding Places from which to Launch a Sneak Attack

Good:

- Up a tree

- Behind a bush

- Around a corner

Bad:

- On top of a distant mountain

- Beneath a giant illuminated arrow with "Look Here" written on it

- A raised platform, surrounded by elephants, cheerleaders and a brass band

CREATE A DISASTER
SURVIVAL KIT

**We'd like to know what you'd put in
your own Disaster Survival Kit . . .**

**Maybe, like Arty, a Bristly-Brain-Basher
(aka toilet brush) is all you need to keep
enemies at bay?**

**Can you invent a more sophisticated
form of weaponry using a toilet roll or
an empty biscuit tin?**

**Or is all you really want some sweets
and a clean t-shirt?**

**Send us a photo of your Ultimate Disaster
Survival Kit and we'll feature it on our website
PLUS UK readers could be in with the chance
of winning a fantastic family day out!**

**Visit www.lbkids.co.uk/disaster
(and find out what the LBKids team have put
in their Disaster Survival Kits)**

R. McGeddon is absolutely sure the world is almost certainly going to probably end very soon. A strange, reclusive fellow – so reclusive, in fact, that no one has ever seen him, not even his mum – he plots his stories using letters cut from old newspapers, then posts them to award-winning author, **Barry Hutchison**, to type up. Barry is not entirely sure why he has been chosen, but he considers it his duty to get R. McGeddon's apocalyptic tales out there. Also, he's too scared to say no.

The suspiciously happy, award-winning illustrator **Jamie Littler** hails from the mysterious, mystical southern lands of England. It is said that the only form of nourishment he needs is to draw, which he does on a constant basis. This could explain why his hair grows so fast. When he is not drawing, which is a rare thing indeed, he spends his time trying to find the drawing pen he has just lost. He is down to his last one. As the sole survivor of the 2008 Tiki Mutant Jellyfish Disaster, Jamie is considered a prime candidate to illustrate the Disaster Diaries.